The Little Wonderer

For future scientists

By Joseph Cordaro
Illustrated by US Illustration

2025

Copyright © 2025 Joseph Cordaro

All rights reserved. This book or any portion thereof may not be reproduced or used in any manner whatsoever without the express written permission of the publisher except for the use of brief quotations in a book review.

First printing, 2025.

To future scientists

May your wonder bring you places beyond your wildest dreams...

-JC

It was a warm summer night when the little wonderer looked up at the stars in awe.

Hydrogen (H)

Helium (He)

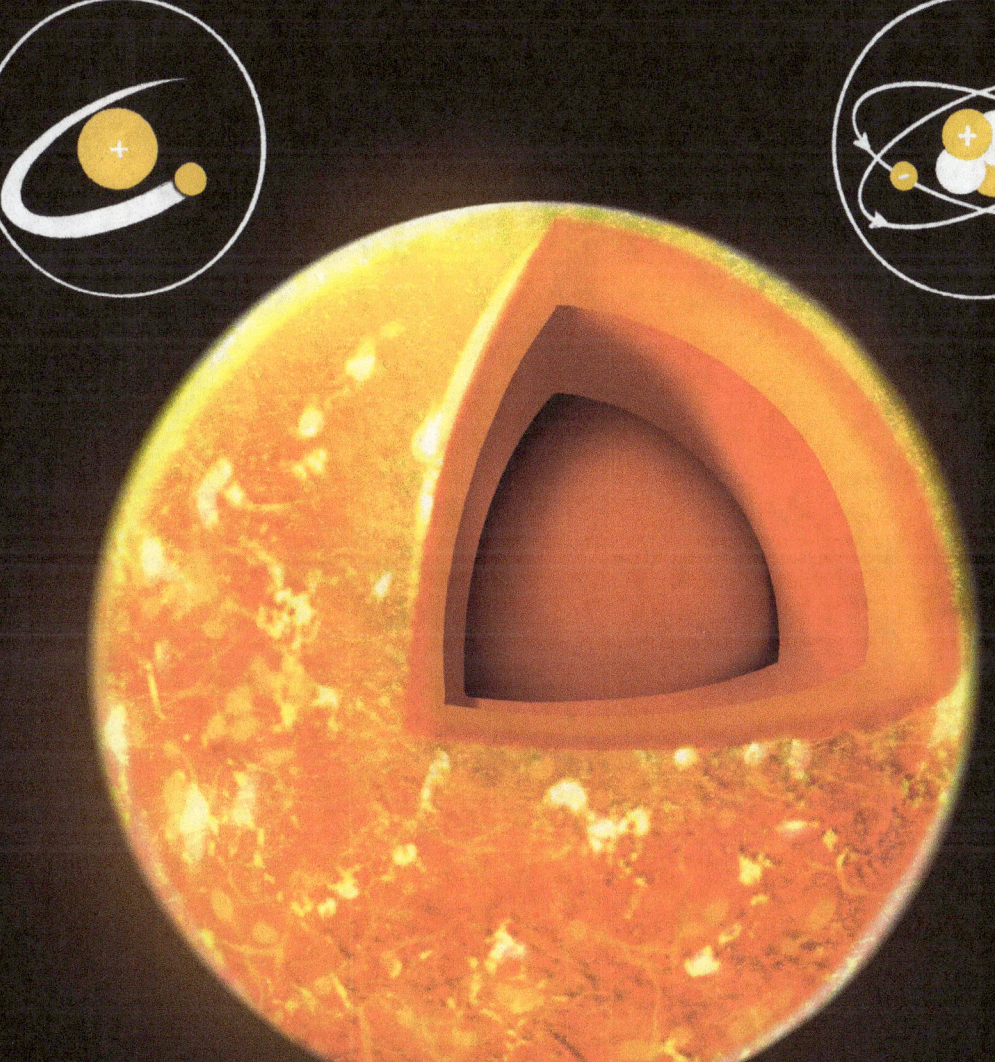

Stars are giant balls of gas, mostly Hydrogen and Helium.

Our star, the Sun, is an ancient star over 4.6 Billion years old!
It is a medium sized star known as a Yellow Dwarf.

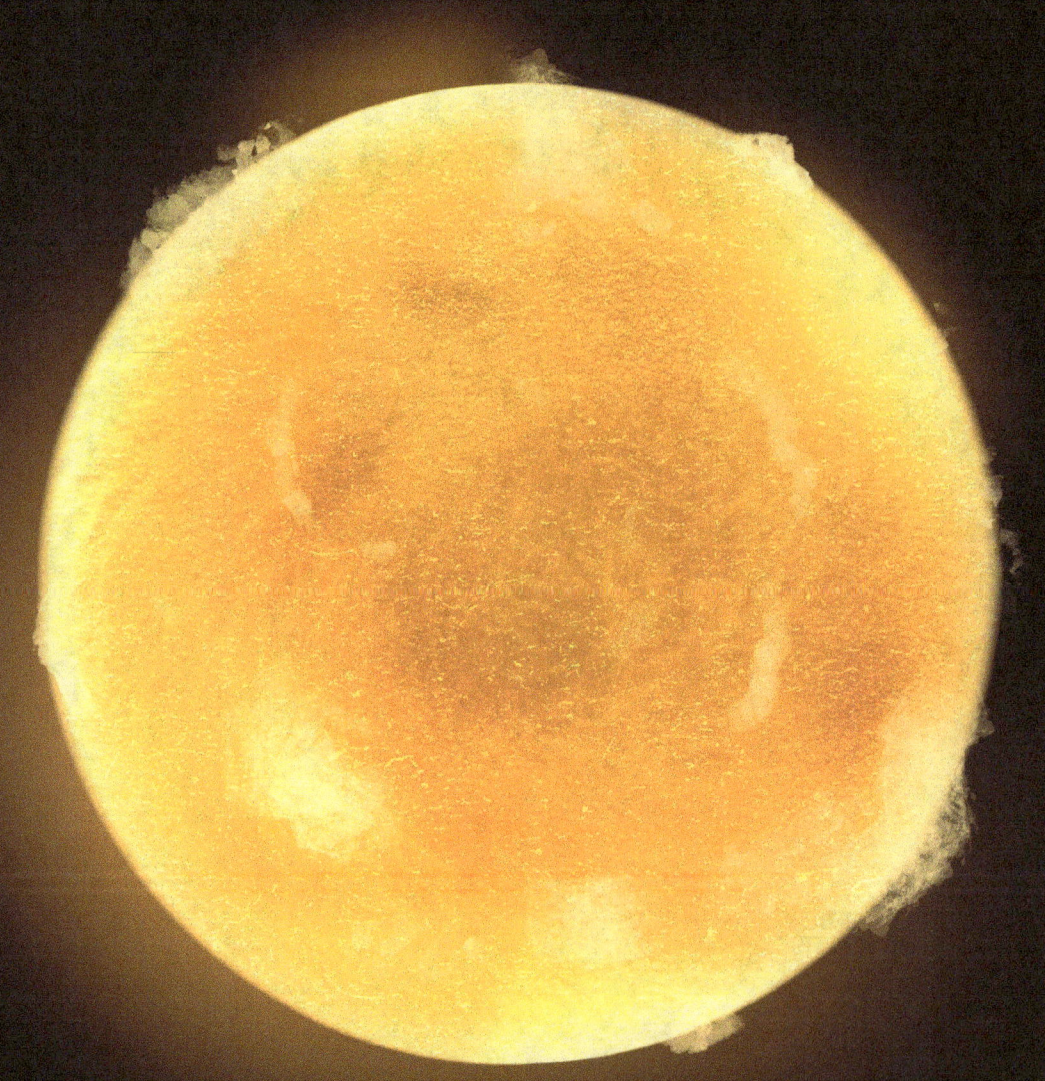

The Sun
Yellow Dwarf

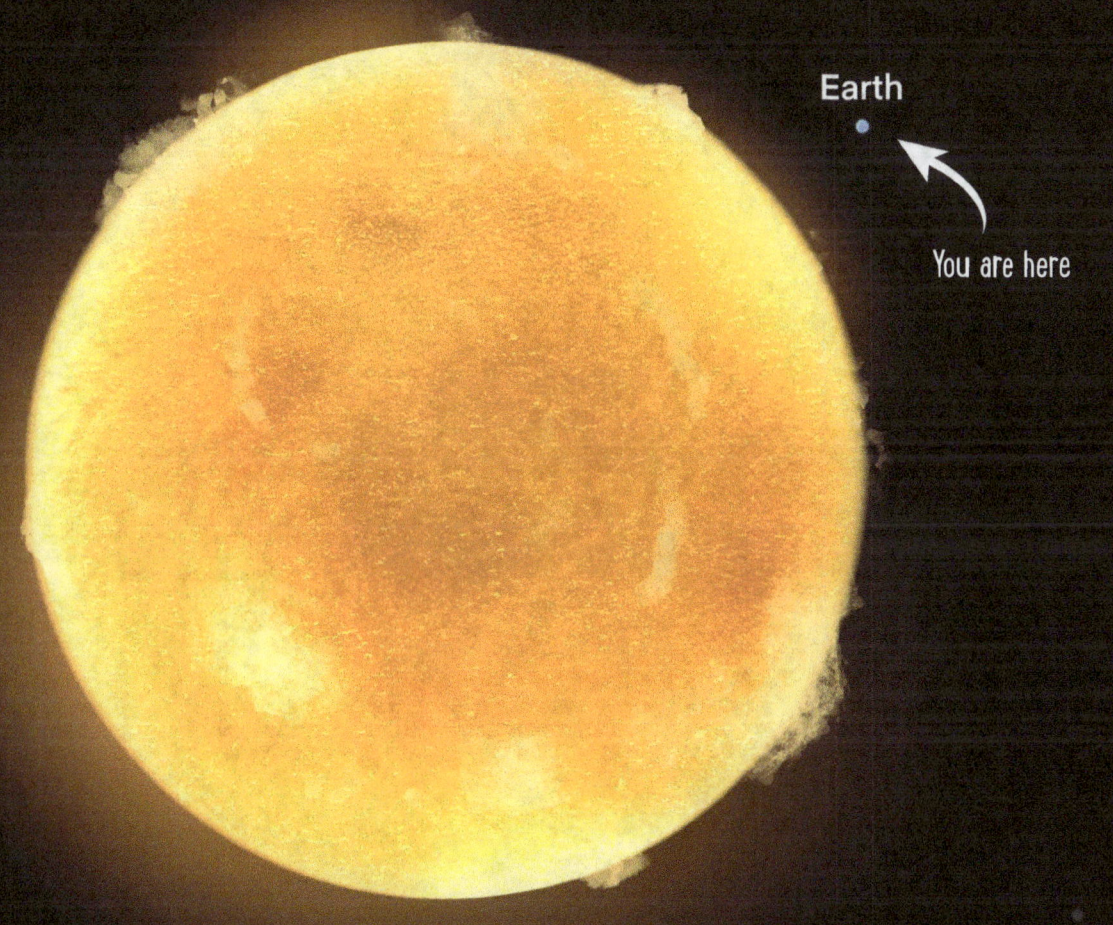

The Sun, is really big...

Earth
← You are here

The Sun

Although the Sun appears yellow or orange in the sky, it is actually white!

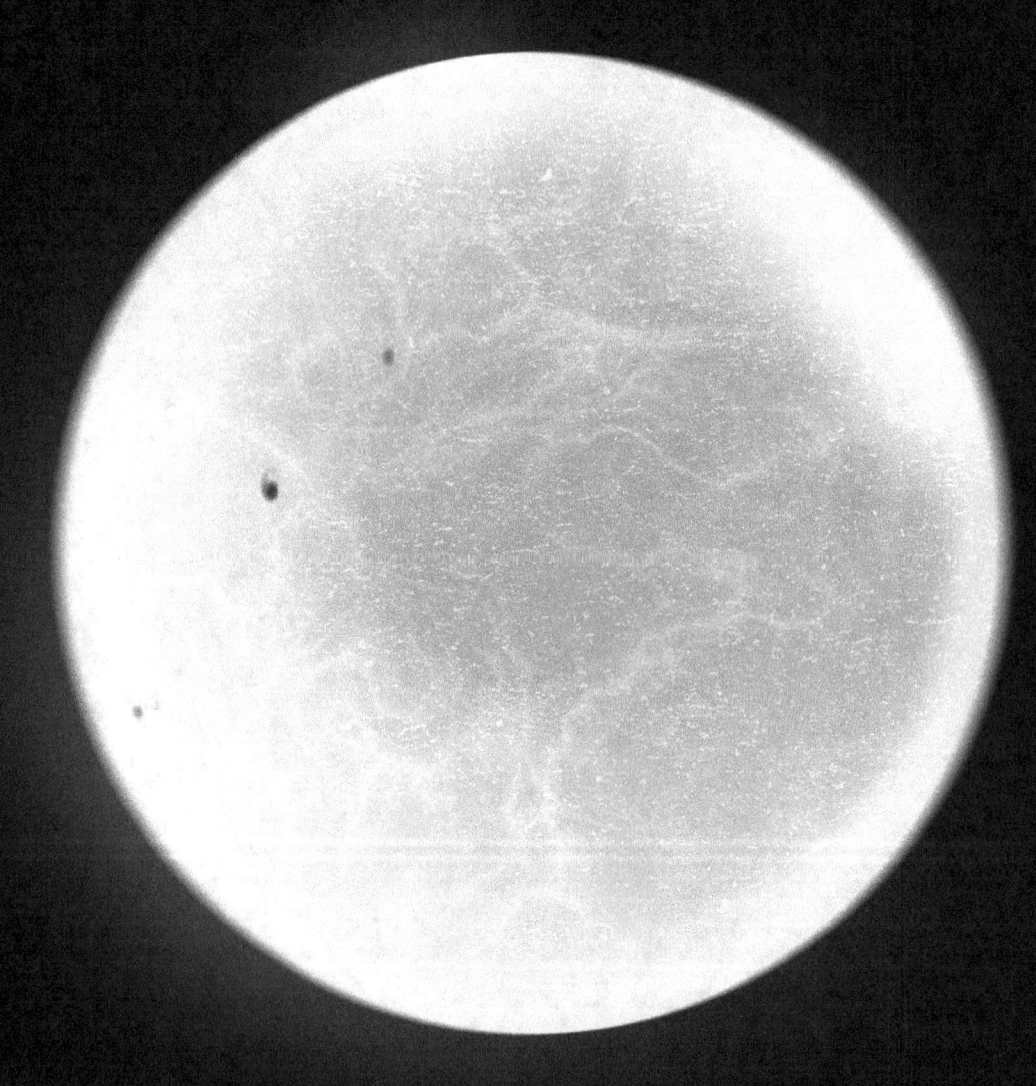

But stars come in many different sizes and colors.

Some stars are really big.

Arcturus
Red Giant

The Sun

12

And some stars are absolutely massive!

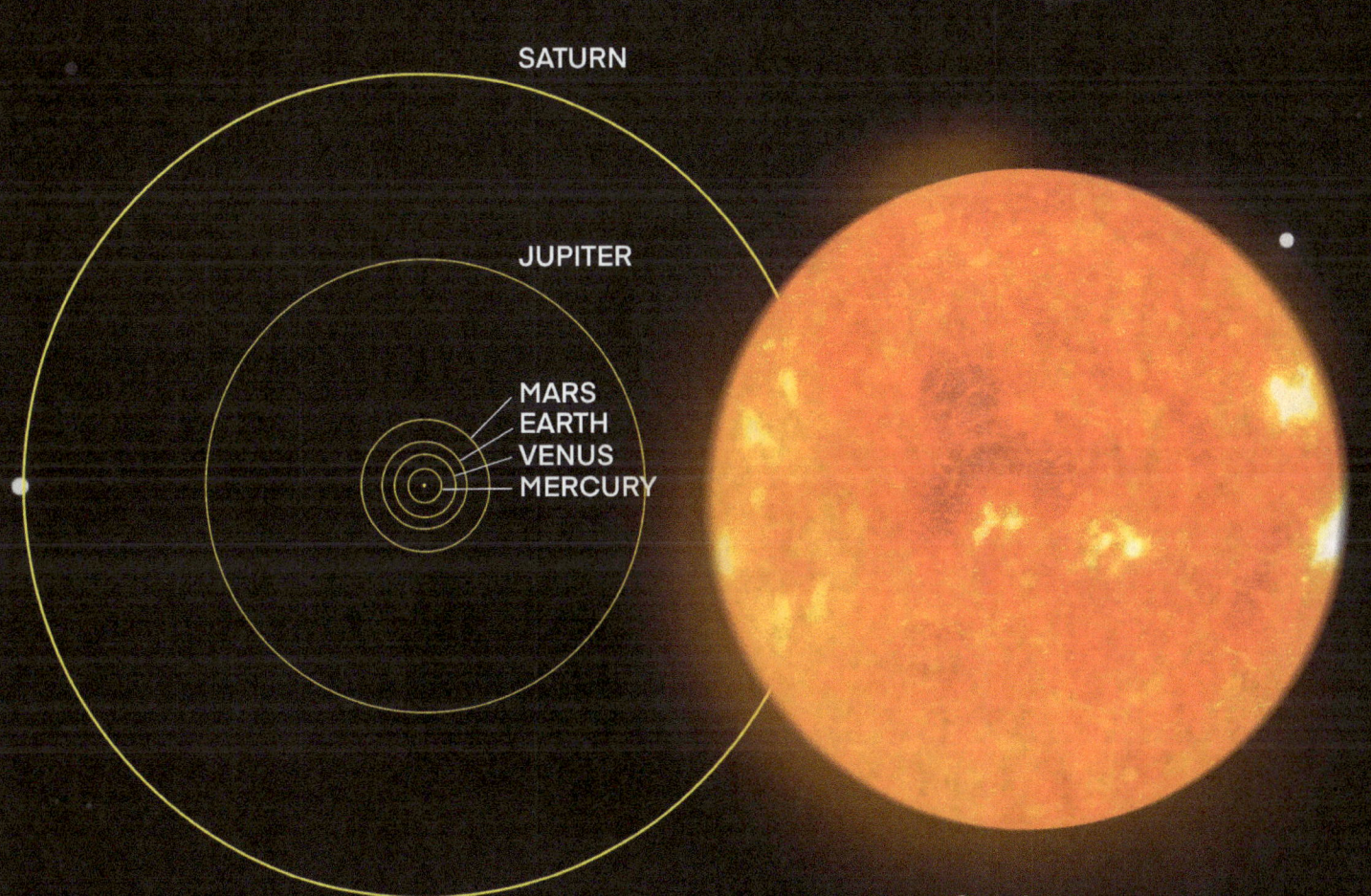

Some stars are small.

Some stars are really hot.

Rigel
Blue Supergiant: 12,000 K (Twice as hot as the Sun)

And some stars are relatively cool.

WISE 0855
Brown Dwarf: 285 K (Cooler than a camp fire)

But the stars are all very far apart.

17

Proxima Centauri
(Closest star to Earth)

4.2 Light Years

Earth

Even the ones in our own back yard are light years away.

But some stars are unfathomably far away!

Earendel
(Farthest known star)

12.9 Billion Light Years

Earth

*Because the Universe is expanding, Earendel is thought to actually be 28 Billion light years away!

Since it takes star light many years to reach us, when you look up at the stars you are seeing them as they were years ago.

Most stars belong to grand galaxies.

Whirlpool Galaxy
(Grand Design Galaxy)

Galaxies are collections of billions of stars!

Andromeda Galaxy

Galaxies are really big and hold a lot of stars.

*Shown: Star densities at different regions of the galaxy.

Our Galaxy: The Milky Way, has over 200 billion stars and is 100,000 light years across!

100,000 Light Years

THE MILKY WAY

It takes the Sun about 230 million years to go around the Milky Way one time.

SUN

This means that the last time the sun was in this location of the galaxy... there were Dinosaurs on Earth!!

The Milky Way is so big that all the stars that you see at night are only a part of this small circle.

*Visible stars in the night sky

The Milky Way is so big that if it was shrunk down to the size of the US, the Sun would be the size of a red blood cell!

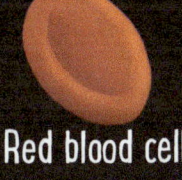
Red blood cell

The Sun

And there are Billions of Galaxies in the Universe!

*Almost every dot on this image is an entire Galaxy!!

All the Carbon in your muscles, the Iron in your blood and the Calcium in your bones was made by the stars.

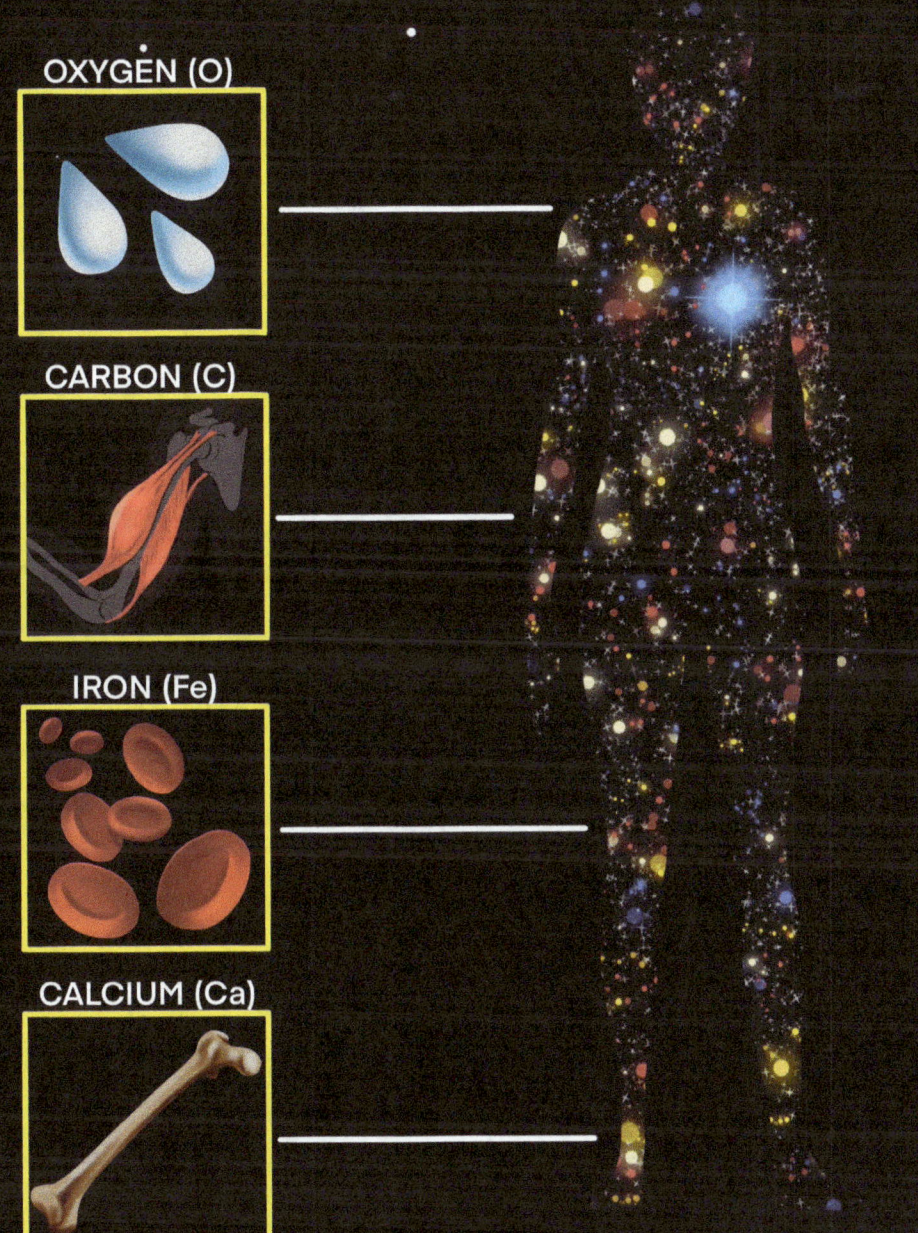

So, when you look up at the stars you should feel big! Because we are made of them!!

The End

www.ingramcontent.com/pod-product-compliance
Lightning Source LLC
LaVergne TN
LVHW060331080526
838201LV00118BA/3039